This Journal Belongs to
MASON E. PIG
A Three Little Pigs Fractured Fairy Tale

written by Jose Cruz
illustrated by Danesh Mohiuddin

PICTURE WINDOW BOOKS
a capstone imprint

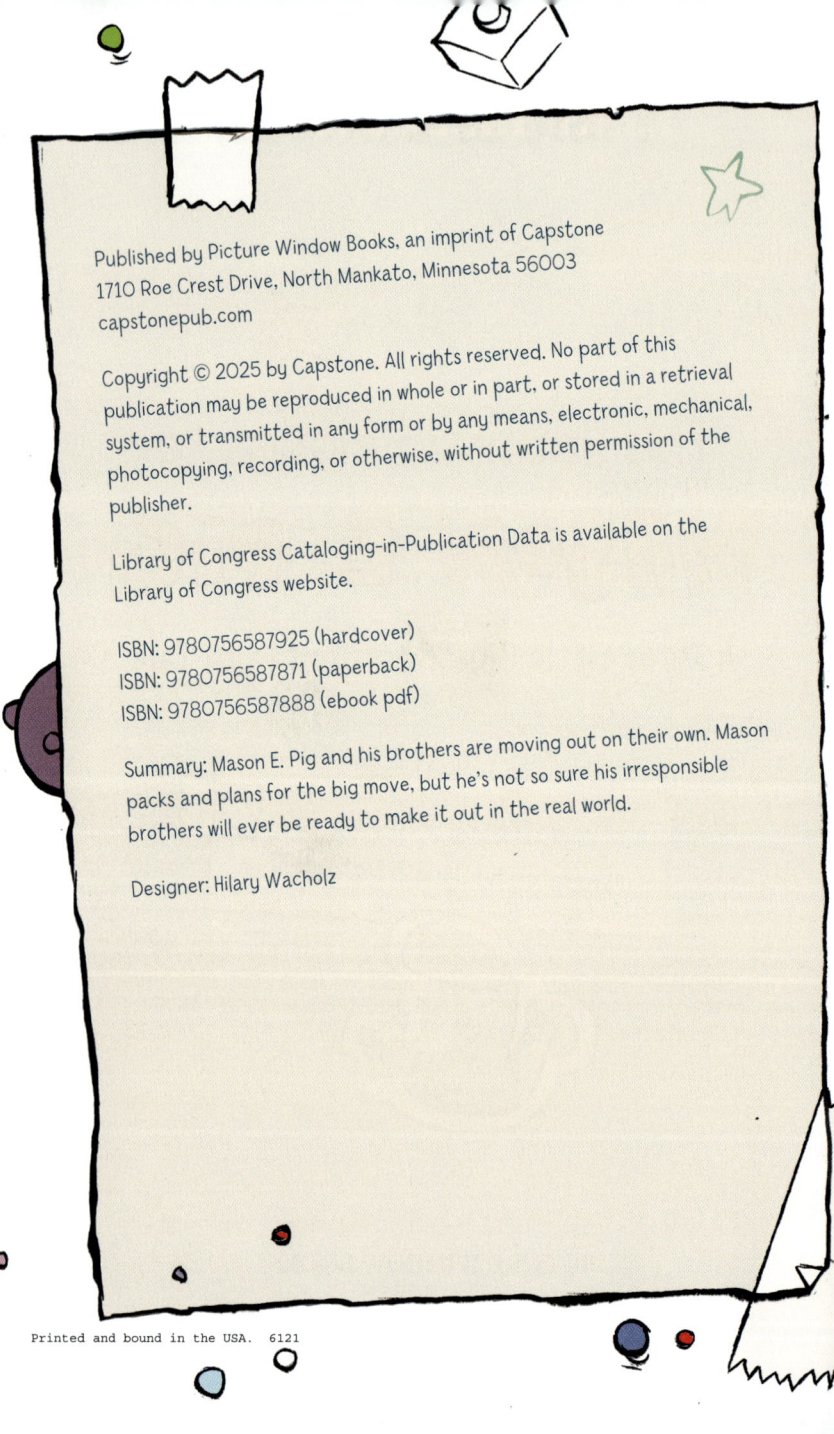

Published by Picture Window Books, an imprint of Capstone
1710 Roe Crest Drive, North Mankato, Minnesota 56003
capstonepub.com

Copyright © 2025 by Capstone. All rights reserved. No part of this publication may be reproduced in whole or in part, or stored in a retrieval system, or transmitted in any form or by any means, electronic, mechanical, photocopying, recording, or otherwise, without written permission of the publisher.

Library of Congress Cataloging-in-Publication Data is available on the Library of Congress website.

ISBN: 9780756587925 (hardcover)
ISBN: 9780756587871 (paperback)
ISBN: 9780756587888 (ebook pdf)

Summary: Mason E. Pig and his brothers are moving out on their own. Mason packs and plans for the big move, but he's not so sure his irresponsible brothers will ever be ready to make it out in the real world.

Designer: Hilary Wacholz

Table of Contents

Moving Time! 4

Me = Mr. Fix-It 9

The Truth 14

Packing Up! 18

Advice from Mama 21

Building Time! 24

House Calls 29

The Straw House Fell! 35

The Stick House Fell! 39

Mystery Solved 43

Tough as Brick? 47

Hayden & Lincoln = Super Brothers! 50

Learning from Lupita 54

Moving Time!

Hello Journal,

My name is Mason E. Pig and I have big news: Mama has just announced that it is time to move!

What does this mean? It means that me and my two brothers, Hayden and Lincoln, are going to find our own houses!

Mama says we are old enough to start living independently now. The world is a big place, she says, and it's about time we start exploring it on our own.

Mama did give us one warning though. She told us to stay away from the Big Bad Wolves. She actually made us a whole diagram describing the animal food chain. As if we could forget! The Big Bad Wolves are a gang of hungry predators with big appetites. And one of their favorite snacks is Little Piggy Sandwiches! **YIKES!**

I can tell you one thing, Journal—I don't plan on getting **ANYWHERE** near a wolf anytime soon!

Journal, there's something else Mama gave me. It was you! Mama said she wanted me to have you so I could write down all the fun adventures I have on my own now.

I promised Mama I would keep track of all my most exciting moments. And this is one of them.

But if I'm going to start telling you all about my life here, I guess I should catch you up on a few things first.

MONDAY
↳ part 2

Me = Mr. Fix-It

If there's one thing you should know about me, Journal, it's this: I am a do-er. What's a *do-er*? A do-er is someone who *does* things.

You see, I'm always taking care of things. I clean the house, I get my homework done, and sometimes I cook dinner for the whole family. (Everyone thinks my macaroni and cheese is the best.)

And even after I get all of that done, I am still doing things. One of my favorite hobbies is working on my building block sets.

Not to brag, but I have 15 finished sets of PORCO blocks in my room. My favorites are the castle, the space station, and the giant dinosaur diorama. I just love snapping those bricks together and creating something new that wasn't there before.

But do you know who isn't a do-er? Either of my two brothers! They barely get anything done at all.

Hayden is my oldest brother—the First Little Pig. He would rather play basketball all day than take out the trash even when Mama has asked him five times.

But Hayden is a real clown. All he has to do is make a silly face or crack a joke and soon Mama is too busy laughing to remember what she asked him to do.

Lincoln is different. He's the middle child—the Second Little Pig. Lincoln prefers to play video games over sports. But he plays them **ALL THE TIME**. It's like the controller is glued to his hands. Mama has to shout over his headset if she wants him to fold his laundry.

Lincoln doesn't make jokes. He whines. **A LOT.** He's always crying about how the level in the game is too hard or how Mama is always interrupting him. He can't do any chores because he's too busy crying about them!

And then there's me—the Third Little Pig. Everyone calls me Mr. Fix-It because of all the things I do. It's a nice name, I guess. I do like to accomplish things.

But if I'm being honest, Journal, it's not all that great. You see, I have a secret . . .

That will have to wait for another day. There's a stack of dirty dishes calling my name. Good night for now, Journal.

Love,
Mason

Hello Journal,

It's been a few days since we've talked. If it's okay with you, I think I'd like to talk about my secret now.

You see, it is true I like to get things finished and do a good job. But the thing is I don't FEEL all that good about it.

There are times when I just don't WANT to be Mr. Fix-It anymore. Do I **ALWAYS** need to be the responsible one in the family? Can't I just relax and let someone else fix things for a change?

But the problem is I **CAN'T** let someone else take charge. If that happens, then the job isn't going to be done right. Or it won't be done at all!

I know this because it's already happened to me. Last Mother's Day was the worst. Hayden and Lincoln promised me they were going to get Mama a present and make her breakfast. Just write the card, they said. That's all you need to do.

Well, guess what? Morning came on **Mother's Day** and there wasn't a single bow or slice of toast to be seen! My brothers said they thought Mother's Day wasn't for another week.

So, I did everything myself. By the time Mama woke up, I had a plate of scrambled eggs, a bunch of flowers from the garden, and a homemade card waiting for her. I signed all our names on the card even though Hayden and Lincoln didn't give me ANY help. All I wanted was for Mama to have a nice day.

And that's the truth, Journal. I'm Mr. Fix-It because I feel like I HAVE to be. Most of the time, I feel like the only person I can depend on is myself.

That's all for today, Journal. I'll talk to you soon.

 Mason

Packing Up!

Hello Journal,

PHEW! Have I been one busy little piggy!

Today, Mama gave us an important mission at breakfast. Mama said even though we might be able to FIND a house in the wild, we should have a plan to BUILD our own house if we need to.

Mama also said we should begin packing our things. I started drawing up a blueprint and writing a checklist right away! The blueprint will help me make sure my house is big and strong enough to live in. And the checklist will help me make sure I don't miss a single thing I need to do.

Here's the beginning of my list:

STUFF I NEED IN MY NEW HOUSE

- My clothes
- My toothbrush
- My bed
- My PORCO sets
- My fountain pens
- My merit badges

In just a few hours I had all these things hitched to a wagon. I was ready to hit the road. Not bad!

But since I completed my mission first, Mama asked me to check on Hayden and Lincoln to see if they needed help.

Surprise, surprise—my brothers had not worked on their moving plans **AT ALL.**

Hayden was too busy perfecting his slam dunk to start packing. And even though Lincoln was building a house in *Swinecraft*, he had no interest in talking about how to find a REAL house. Ugh!

I've got a bad feeling my brothers' jobs are going to fall on Mr. Fix-It again.

Advice from Mama

Hello Journal,

I was starting to feel real upset about all of this earlier. But as I was writing the last entry, I felt Mama's hand on my shoulder. She told me to come with her and together we began getting my brothers' things ready.

Between folding Hayden's jerseys and making peanut butter sandwiches for Lincoln, I asked Mama if she really believed we were ready to live on our own. She said she did. I was

"Even Hayden and Lincoln?" I asked. Mama said she thinks all three of her boys are capable of great things.

Mama is a teacher at MacDonald Elementary. She is always saying those kinds of things to us and her students at school.

Mama says we can achieve anything so long as we push ourselves. But she said greatness comes at different times for different people. She told me not to worry about my brothers so much and to have more faith in them.

YEAH RIGHT. I already tried that. But Mama just gave me a hug and said everything will work out in the end.

I may not believe in my brothers, Journal, but I do believe in Mama.

Love,
Mason

Building Time!

Hello Journal,

Well, here we are! The Big Day. The last week has really flown by.

Mama and I managed to get everything packed for Hayden and Lincoln. (They helped zip up their luggage.)

We all said our goodbyes and gave lots of hugs. Then we started down the road with our wagons.

Soon the road went off in three separate paths. I asked Hayden and Lincoln what their plans were. They both shrugged and gave me a big IDK face. **UNBELIEVABLE**.

I started feeling that old worry again, but then I remembered Mama's advice. I wished them both good luck. I asked them to write to me once they settled in their new houses.

Then I took one path from the main road and my brothers took the two others.

It was real now. We were on our own.

I tried to focus by looking at my checklist. The next item was "Find a good location." That came easy! The path led to a beautiful meadow. It made the perfect spot for my dream home.

The next item on the list was "Build the house." That would be a little trickier, but I had planned ahead.

A few days ago, I placed a special order for a life-size set of PORCO blocks. I took them down from my wagon, rolled out my blueprint for the house, and got to work.

I carefully snapped each block in place, double-checking my work along the way. It took a long time—almost all day—but at the end my house was complete. It is **BEAUTIFUL**. Probably my best work yet. I'm actually writing this entry from my new bedroom.

Speaking of bed, it's time I took a rest. Good night, Journal.

Love,
Mason

House Calls

Hello Journal,

It's been a few days in my new house, and I am so **HAPPY.** So happy I almost missed the postcards that came this morning. They were from Hayden and Lincoln, and they showed the addresses of their new houses.

I almost spit out my cereal when I read that! They had houses already? I couldn't believe it. I felt the worry coming back, but I told myself to relax. I decided to head over to see how they were doing.

What I found was pretty surprising, Journal. And a little strange too.

I visited Hayden first. When I saw the house, I didn't know whether to laugh or cry. Hayden's house is made of **STRAW**. Straw, Journal! It's sitting in the middle of a barnyard. It would only take one strong wind to send that house flying away!

Bad idea!

But I tried to be nice. I asked Hayden how long it took him to build it. He said he didn't build it. He found it just like that in the barnyard.

That made me worry a little bit. But then that's when I started seeing them. Little clumps of gray fur on the floor and in the straw. Hayden doesn't have gray fur!

That wasn't all. There were these plastic wrappers lying around too. It looked like they came from some kind of snack bar. But my brothers hate snack bars! They won't touch them!

I didn't stick around long after that. I hurried over to Lincoln's house.

Lincoln's house is in the middle of the woods. Do you want to guess what his house is made of? **STICKS**. A little better than straw, but not much. When I was there, I kept thinking how easy it'd be to knock the whole place down.

I asked Lincoln the same question, but I knew what he would say. He had found the stick house there in the woods, same as Hayden finding the straw house.

But that wasn't the worst part.

I found the same clumps of gray fur and snack-bar wrappers in Lincoln's house! Too bizarre. Why would that stuff be in **BOTH** places?

When I left, I told Hayden and Lincoln to reach out if they needed anything.

I think my worry is getting to me, Journal. Because there was one more thing that upset me during my visits today.

After I left both brothers' houses, I could have sworn I heard someone **HOWLING** in the distance!

The Straw House Fell!

Journal,

Something **TERRIBLE** has happened!

Hayden's straw house has fallen!

Actually, it didn't fall all by itself.

That's the worst part. Hayden told me

that it was **BLOWN** away—by a

BIG BAD WOLF!!!

Let me try to get all of this in order . . .

I woke up to Hayden pounding on my door. He told me it all happened so fast. He was doing his morning stretches when he heard the Big Bad Wolf trying to break into the straw house. And the Wolf was shouting, "Get out of that house!"

When Hayden hid away just like Mama taught us, the Wolf began to huff and puff. Next thing Hayden knew, the whole straw house was blown right over his head. That's when he ran wee-wee-wee all the way over to my house.

Hayden says he didn't see much of the Big Bad Wolf, but he did notice it was wearing sneakers. I wonder what that could mean.

Hang on, Journal. I hear someone calling. Oh my goodness—it's Lincoln!

The Stick House Fell!

I'm really starting to worry bad, Journal. Lincoln is over here now too. And the same thing has just happened to him!

He told me he was on the final boss level of *Mortal Wombat* when the Big Bad Wolf started pounding on **HIS** door! And it was shouting the same thing: "Get out of that house!"

So, Lincoln hid away, but it wasn't long before the Wolf huffed and puffed and blew that stick house away. Once that happened Lincoln ran as fast as his legs could carry him to my place.

He said he just got a quick glimpse of the Wolf as he was running away. He said it looked like the Wolf was wearing a sweatband around its head.

Sneakers and sweatbands? I don't remember Mama telling us Big Bad Wolves wore anything like that.

It's all so strange. What could it mean?

I'm just glad Hayden and Lincoln made it here safely. Hopefully the Wolf wasn't smart enough to follow—

Hang on. My brothers are shouting.

OH NO, JOURNAL!

THE WOLF IS HERE!!!

↳ part 3

Mystery Solved

↑
by me ☺

OH NO OH NO OH NO

I can't believe this is happening, Journal. The Big Bad Wolf is right outside my door!

Good news is that it looks like my PORCO bricks are stronger than straw and sticks. The Wolf is huffing and puffing outside, but the house isn't going anywhere. Hooray!

My brothers and I are watching from the living room window as I write this. We can see the Big Bad Wolf clearly from here, but I don't think it can see us. Hayden and Lincoln were right— the Wolf is wearing sneakers and a sweatband. It looks like it's dressed for the gym. How weird is that?!

Wait a minute. I just noticed something. The Wolf has something in the pockets of its shorts. It looks like the same snack-bar wrappers I found in the straw and stick houses.

And the Wolf has gray fur, just like those clumps I found in the houses too! What could this mean?

What was it Hayden and Lincoln said the Wolf shouted at their doors? "Get out of that house!" Could it be . . . could it be the Wolf was actually shouting "Get out of **MY** house!"?

If that's true, Journal, it can only mean one thing: Hayden and Lincoln stole their houses from the Big Bad Wolf!!!

Tough as Brick?

Journal,

This may be the last entry I write for a long time. I'm in my bedroom right now. I can't stop crying, so I'm sorry for getting your pages wet.

I just got done yelling at my brothers. I told them what I figured out about the Big Bad Wolf.

My brothers promised they had no idea the houses belonged to the Wolf. But it doesn't matter. I was so angry and upset I just kept shouting at them.

I told them how I'm sick of cleaning up all their messes. How I don't want to be Mr. Fix-It anymore. I even said Mama was wrong about them. They're not ready to live on their own. They never will be! And now there's a hungry Wolf at our door and it's **ALL THEIR FAULT!**

So, I said I was done figuring out their problems. That's when I ran in here and closed the door.

I'd rather sit here with you, Journal. You're a better friend than my brothers are.

Hold on. It's gotten very quiet outside. I don't hear the Wolf huffing and puffing anymore. What happened?

Wait—is that the front door opening? Voices . . . And now footsteps coming this way?

Oh no, Journal. The doorknob to the bedroom is turning. I think this is the end!

Hayden & Lincoln = Super Brothers!

Hello Journal,

I can't believe I'm about to write this next entry. I think it'll even surprise **YOU**.

When the bedroom door opened, Hayden and Lincoln were there . . . and so was the Big Bad Wolf! I was about to scream my little head off, but my brothers told me it was okay.

We weren't going to be eaten!

Then I was confused. My brothers saw this and explained. After I had yelled at them, Hayden and Lincoln realized how much they had been relying on me. They thought I *liked* fixing things because I was good at it. But they understood this whole mess had happened because of them.

So, they agreed to **OPEN** THE FRONT DOOR AND INVITE THE WOLF **INSIDE**.

Journal, I was speechless. I could **NEVER** imagine myself doing something as brave as that.

Hayden and Lincoln apologized to the Wolf for forcing her out. They said it wasn't right for them to just take something without even asking. They thought they could skip the hard work and do what was easy. But by doing that they ended up hurting the Wolf.

I should really stop saying "the Wolf." That's not her name. She told us her name is Lupita.

AFTERNOON → part 2

Learning from Lupita

Let me tell you about Lupita, Journal.

Lupita is a workout wolf. That's why she's always dressed for the gym. She said she used to be one of the Big Bad Wolves. They were her pack. But Lupita never liked Little Piggy Sandwiches. She liked getting protein from her snack bars instead.

The other wolves didn't like that Lupita disagreed with them. So they left her all by herself. SO SAD.

Since Lupita was on her own now, she had to find a new home. She built the straw house first. While she was out exercising, Hayden came and moved in.

Lupita was too shocked and sad to ask for it back. She went to build another house for herself in the woods. The stick house Lincoln moved into! After that, Lupita said all her feelings got so big that she **BLEW UP** a little bit. (Boy, do I know what that's like!)

After I heard her story, Journal, I did something I learned from Mama. I gave Lupita a big hug and told her everything would be okay. And my brothers did the same!

I feel like the future seems less scary now. I feel like I don't just have to depend on myself. I have a whole **AWESOME TEAM** working with me! Hayden and Lincoln proved they had greatness in them. They needed time to find it, just like Mama said.

I needed time too. Time to learn how to let things go and let other people do amazing things for a change. I have to admit, Journal—it feels really good.

You've been a great friend this whole time, Journal. So patient and such a good listener! But now you need a rest. I've been writing an awful lot this past month.

Turns out Mama was right after all, Journal. Things really did work out in . . .

← Dino!

GLOSSARY

accomplish (uh-KOM-plish)—to finish successfully

bizarre (bi-ZAR)—out of the ordinary

blueprint (BLOO-print)—a plan for building

diorama (DY-oh-ram-uh)—a model that shows a situation, such as a historical event or animals in their natural environment, in a way that looks real

independently (in-di-PEN-duhnt-lee)—to be free of being controlled by someone or something

protein (PROH-teen)—a substance found in certain foods that are an important part of a diet

speechless (SPEECH-less)—not able to speak

HOW TO CREATE YOUR OWN JOURNAL

Would you like to have your very own journal like Mason? Journals are a great way to keep track of the important moments in your life. Follow the steps below to get started on your journaling adventure!

1. Find something to use as your journal.

Anything can be used as a journal. It's best if all the pages can be kept together, like in a binder or folder. Using a notebook is one of the simplest ways to start. Only have paper? No problem! You can connect the sheets using staples, paper clips, or even yarn to make your journal.

2. Think about things you can write about.

Did anything happen today that you'd like to record? Something that surprised you, excited you, or made you wonder? Mason also wrote about things that were upsetting him. You may find that writing these down will help you feel better.

3. Start creating!

Don't worry about spelling or grammar. This journal is for you, so write it in the way you want to. And it doesn't just have to be words. Draw pictures or comics, add stickers, and glue photographs to make your journal come to life.

TALK ABOUT IT

- Mason doesn't think his brothers will be able to accomplish anything at the beginning of the story, but then changes his mind when he sees what they're capable of doing. Talk about a time when you weren't sure about someone else's abilities but were later surprised by them.

- Discuss how Mason's story is similar to the traditional tale of the Three Little Pigs. In what ways are the stories different?

- Hayden and Lincoln show great bravery at the end of the story when they face "the Big Bad Wolf." Have you ever faced a challenge before where you had to be brave? How did you feel after it happened?

WRITE ABOUT IT

- Mason's journal is from the point of view of the Third Little Pig. Write a journal entry from the point of view of one of Mason's brothers. How would the story change if it was written from Lupita's point of view?

- During the story Mason solves a mystery using clues he finds in the straw and stick houses. Draw a picture of a scene that has clues hidden inside it. Write the solution to the mystery on the opposite side of the page and see if anyone can guess what is going on in your picture.

- Mama gives Mason advice that helps him through a difficult time. Write about a time you had a problem and received help from a family member, friend, or teacher. What did they say or do to make you feel better?

ABOUT THE AUTHOR

Jose Cruz is an elementary school media specialist based in southwest Florida. His journalism and short fiction have appeared in print and online, including best-of collections.

ABOUT THE ILLUSTRATOR

Danesh Mohiuddin's list of creative pursuits includes comic books, political cartooning, designing toys and games, and freelance illustrating for leading publishers. Danesh was born in India and grew up in Dubai. He now lives in Toronto, Ontario, with his wife and children.